It's New Year's!

Kylie Wyman

Illustrated by Monique Machut

Kylie Wyman

Published by Orange Hat Publishing 2023
PB ISBN: 9781645384779
HC ISBN: 9781645384762

It's New Year's!
Written by Kylie Wyman
Illustrated by Monique Machut

orangehatpublishing.com

For Chad, Ava, and Penelope,
my New Year's Crew

Decorations shine
all through the house.
Kids playing with toys,
Mom's in her new blouse.

The holidays are over;
they've all come to an end.
But now wait just a moment;
grab your family, your friend.

One last celebration
where we close out the year.
There's one last holiday,
and it is almost here!

Each year is twelve months;
we go through them all.
It ends on New Year's Eve
with the drop of a ball.

Head out to the stores,
pick out a few things:
streamers, noisemakers,
and glassware to clink.

Make a party hat;
shiny crowns work too!
Cut some confetti
with your New Year's crew.

It's almost the day
the wait was all for.
Tonight's one last night,
the last one before...

Go get your family;
grab a neighbor or friend.
Have a party at home
or find one to attend.

Tonight we celebrate;
tonight we are merry!
Dinner, games, and dancing
with drinks that are berry!

It's time for the countdown;
the year's almost done.
Ten, nine, eight, seven, six,
five, four, three, two, one…

Happy
New Year!

The new year has arrived!
Celebrating was fun.
It feels like it's over,
but it's just now begun!

What does that mean?
What's just begun?
Gather in close
to tell everyone.

NEW means a refresh,
to start over again.
You set a new goal,
maybe two, maybe ten!

Sit down together;
make sure you are near.
Listen to each other,
and be ready to cheer.

Think back on the year.
What made you feel proud?
What did you learn?
Share it out loud.

When it's your turn to go
and you know what to share,
be confident, be loud;
then get out of your chair.

Did you help out your sister?
Did you try to be kind?
Did you work on listening?
Or on growing your mind?

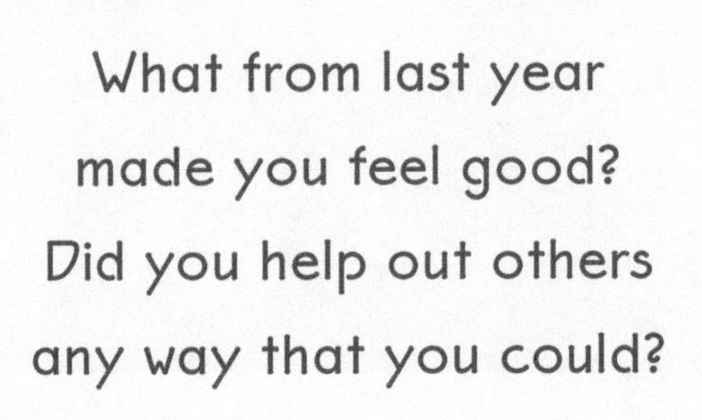

What from last year
made you feel good?
Did you help out others
any way that you could?

It's amazing to think of
all those incredible things.
It's exciting to look toward
what this new year will bring!

Now that you've thought of
the great things you've done,
start looking forward,
get ready to run!

What goal is your next?
Your next to work on?
There's no limit on what;
every day's a new dawn.

How can you grow?

What can you learn?

This is YOUR year!
NOW it's YOUR turn!

So write down your goals
or shout them out loud.
Whisper them quiet
or share with your crowd.

It's the new year! It is here!
Celebrations are done.
It's time for the best *YOU*.
Make it a special one!

It's New Year's!

ACTIVITIES

Can You Find...

Readers, can you find our New Year's stars hidden on each page?

First, follow the countdown of stars going from page one to page ten. There are ten stars on page one, nine stars on page two, eight stars on page three... all the way down to one star on page ten, just before New Year's hits on the next page!

Next, on each page after New Year's arrives, can you find all ten stars hidden in the pictures?

Last, can you find where our two characters' stuffed cow and elephant are on each page?

Good luck!

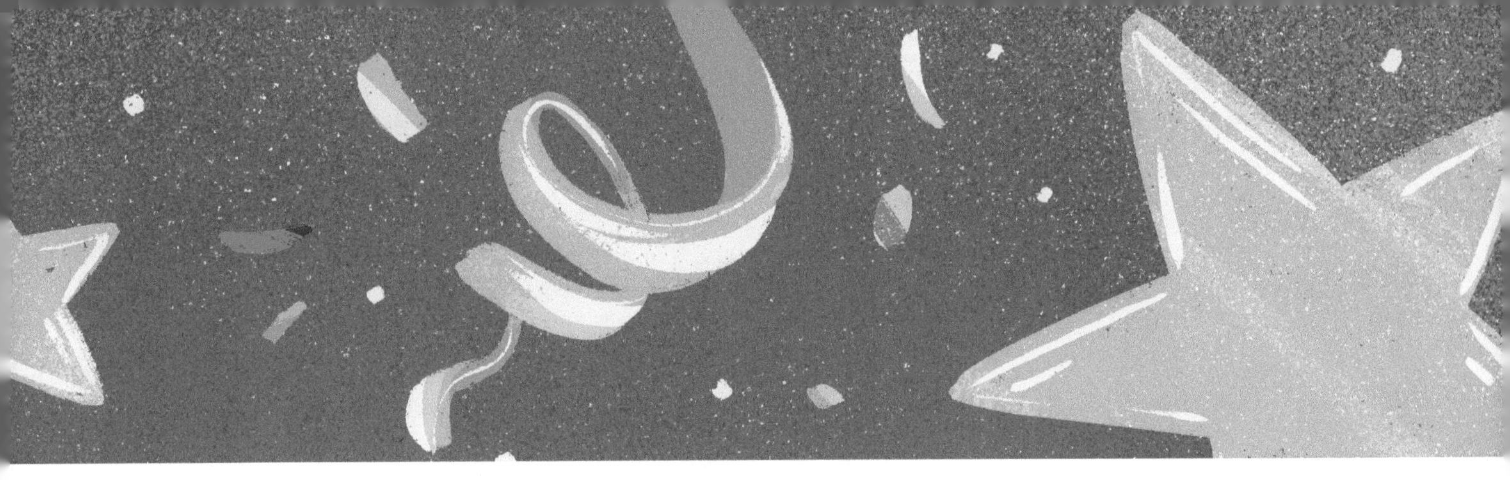

Later Letters

What are your dreams for the new year? Write letters to your "later" self about what your dreams and goals are, and what you want to accomplish this year!

Later Letters can be a family activity for kids and adults alike! Letters can be long or short, filled with words, or even filled with pictures for the littlest family members. Once your letters are complete, seal them in an envelope (you can decorate those too) and store them away with your holiday decorations until next New Year's Eve!

Wall of Wonders

Your family's Wall of Wonders is a special place in your home to hold your family's wishes and wonders for the new year. What is everyone hoping for in the new year? What questions do you have that you hope to discover the answers to?

First, decide together where your Wall of Wonders is going to be. It can be a whole wall, a door, a cabinet — anywhere you can think of and any size that you can fit! Once you have your spot chosen, decide when you want to complete your Wall of Wonders.

Does your family want to make and finish it on New Year's Day? Or maybe just the first week of January? You might also choose to use the full month of January to add new wishes and wonders to your wall.

Next, plan how you will add your wishes and wonders. You can use a poster board, hang up some craft paper, or go simple with sticky notes (it is fun to give each family member their own color for notes). Now that your plan is in place, get started making those New Year's wishes and asking those New Year's wonders!

And don't forget to stop by your wall throughout the year. If someone accomplishes something from the wall or one of their wishes comes true, celebrate together! You can add special stickers or draw stars on your wall to signify that achievement. The options are endless! If a wonder is figured out, add that on there too!

Triumph Tree

A Triumph Tree is also a special place in your home to go to, much like a Wall of Wonders, but this one is used to post family triumphs made throughout the year. When a goal is met, an achievement is made, a promise is kept, or a success is won, your family can add it to your tree!

To make your family's Triumph Tree, start by finding some paper. It can be craft paper, construction paper, printer paper, or wrapping paper. Taping different papers together works too! Then draw the outline of a tree. You can use any type of tree here. If you choose a pine tree, then each time you add a triumph, you will add them to the inside. If you choose something like a maple or oak tree, you can draw branches and make each triumph a leaf that you add to the tree. Get creative! Have fun with it!

Then, throughout the year, every time someone in your family has a triumph, add it to your tree. On New Year's Eve next year, get together and read through some of your family's successes from the year!

This activity can also be made using a jar. Each time a family member has a triumph for the year, write it down and put that triumph into the jar!

Printed in the USA
CPSIA information can be obtained
at www.ICGtesting.com
JSHW042150221123
52177JS00006B/13
9781645384762